Richard Bloss is CEO of the ProfoMedia Press Agency.

With two other books to his name already, including *The Russian Tourist Guide to London*, published by *Russian Mind Magazine* – Richard handles the PR for other authors, as well as writing critical business articles.

About a Dog is a new departure for him.

Dedication

To Ann, Zoe, Ben, Boh the cat and, of course, Barney.

Richard Bloss

ABOUT A DOG

AUSTIN MACAULEY
PUBLISHERS LTD.

Graphics/artwork by Ben Bloss

A CIP catalogue record for this title is available from the British Library.

ISBN 9781786296368 (Paperback)
ISBN 9781786296375 (Hardback)
ISBN 9781786296382 (E-Book)

www.austinmacauley.com

First Published (2016)
Austin Macauley Publishers Ltd.
25 Canada Square
Canary Wharf
London
E14 5LQ

Acknowledgments

I would like to thank my family for their support and for indulging me in my dream; my wife, Ann, for reading through the initial drafts and making sure I was aware of every single spelling mistake.
But the biggest thanks go to my son Ben whose fantastic artwork made the book come alive.

Contents

Chapter One

The Discovery – How to buy a dog that you never knew you wanted

The road from Plymouth to Tavistock takes you out across the moors; past the little cafe that never seemed to make any sense, but now is a refurbished drop off point for tourists before they cross the cattle grid into Dartmoor, and then bearing left at Yelverton and the signs for the National Trust – and then starts to wind down eventually descending into Tavy.

Tavistock itself has mixed identity, never knowing if it is a feeder station for Plymouth, i.e. people commuting – or whether it is a 'Des Res' like Totnes. I think the fact that it no longer has a train station has resigned or consigned it to the former category.

And then you have some choices. At Tavistock, if you want to travel further, you hit an arborescence of possibilities, each road getting more windy, more narrow, and more obtuse. Local drivers whizz by. You and I, on the other hand, have no clue. What we do know is that 'The Old Farm' is in a little village where you take the road towards Okehampton, but cut off before you get to Mary Tavy, and then down into some village, where I am not sure people have ever discovered telephones, and then after a sharp right, you go up the hill, but it is single track, so be careful, and the Farm should be on the left, with a white gate.

Oh, that's easy then. There is no GPS and your iPhone does not get a Wi-Fi signal. Your Sat Nav has that annoying female habit of screeching "NO! I said LEFT!"

You are by that time several hundred yards past "the turning on your left". There is no space to turn round. You carry on into the next village, find someone's entrance to do a quick 'U-ey', – and then speed back, remembering that – this time – the unmarked turning is on your RIGHT.

You carry on like this for what seems another twenty minutes, but actually really is twenty minutes, with ever increasing slowness. Until there it is.

The Old Farm really does have a white gate. It is a real Farm. There is just enough space to pull my Volvo into the drive entrance and I am met by the most shaggy and unkempt dog I have ever seen. He is nearly blind and he is dirty, and he sidles up to me as I get out of the car, and I have this overwhelming urge to a) give him the most enormous hug (he clearly needs love) – and b) brush his hair and give him some stern advice about male grooming. But he is a dog. He will not understand about Ted Baker Grooming. Maybe Ted Baker will indeed open a facility for doggy grooming, but that's for another day. All I want to say is that this shaggy unkempt old mangy animal has a look of pity in his eyes that brings out all my female side, and I'm a bloke. I'm not supposed to have 'female sides'.

"Oh, that's our Outdoor Dog," says the voice. The farm owner opens his house stable door and introduces himself. I am not sure what an Outdoor Dog actually is, so I let the unsaid question pass, and I nod as if all is clear.

"Right," I say.

"You must be here for the puppy." It is a statement not a question. I suppose I must be. Nobody else could find this bloody place.

"Well, you'd better come in."

The farmer introduces me to his wife, who takes me into one of the internal rooms of their house, which smells of pee, and there in front of me, are six scampering bundles of humanity, all vying for their mum's attention, – who is languishing on the floor and suckling her litter of puppies.

The puppies run all over my shoes, some of them looking up at me with a sort of strange sense of "Who is this person, Mum?" look in their eyes, and then get back to the real business of feeding. Except one.

This little animal starts to climb up my leg. He is grey, mottled, and cute beyond words, with bright eyes and the biggest tongue I have ever seen. I hold him up and he gives me an enormous lick. Nobody has ever shown me such a gesture of unsolicited attention before. I pick him up and he snuggles into my arms and looks up at me with big longing eyes and what has to be a smile. The little animal can only be about a foot long and here I am trying to communicate with … a dog. I have this overwhelming urge to give him a lick back.

This is absolutely bloody ridiculous. It is redolent of Hugh Grant in the Nick Hornby movie. This sort of thing just does not happen to fully grown adult blokes. First – we don't get emotional, ever. Second – what on earth do we do with puppies once we get them home and the novelty wears off? We can hardly take them back. Well perhaps we can but they probably have rules and laws against this sort of thing now, so let's say we can't. And finally – what on earth persuaded me that having a dog was a good idea in the first place?

The farmer's wife looks on lovingly;

"He's really taken to you, hasn't he!" she opines enthusiastically.

This must be the 'closing' part of the sales process. Perhaps all puppies are trained to lick their prospects; it's part of the deal. If they let you lick them, then that's the 'close'… I feel bad about being so cynical but here is this little guy, about to leave his mum, who he will never see again, and his brothers and his sisters, and come to live with some strange grown up person who, for all he knows, may be a supplier to a local Chinese restaurant (apologies, I didn't mean it, it comes from that Gryff Rees-Jones and Mel Smith joke, "a dog is not just for Christmas – as our friends in China say, with a little bit of luck there will be some left over for Boxing day…" How sick! Sorry).

But he continues to look up at me. And I have this feeling that I am going to be the one to look after this little chap. I have been chosen.

"We just have to sort out the invoice!" continues the wife. I am in a daze by this time; it is all happening too fast. As if I am in another world, I am looking down on myself fishing out some £400.00 smackers from my pocket, in twenties, which I see myself handing to the wife. Another sucker, hah!

But it just does not feel that way. In no time at all, I am saying goodbye to the blind and mangy dog outside who gives me a sort of smile and continues to hobble around, whilst I get in my car. The puppy nestles down in my lap as I engage into reverse, I hear the parking beeps sound once or twice, I switch into first and then second and them I am away.

The whole process takes about twenty minutes and something has happened that I never thought ever could take place in my pressured and black life. I have fallen in love with a dog.

Chapter Two

The Background – What makes a grown adult go buy a dog in the first place?

I have never liked dogs. Ever since I was five years old, when some ghastly dog knocked me off my bicycle as I journeyed to my little junior school, I have always known that dogs and dog lovers are a strange race, sadistic.

Couples who have dogs usually never have children. I used to have friends, a gay couple in fact, who let their dogs (plural) sit at the dining table and eat with them. They (the dogs) would lick their plates clean. I only ate with them once. I never saw them put the dishes into a dishwasher and I was too terrified to ask, "Who the hell – if you don't mind – washes the bloody plates?"

And I have relations who have enormous dogs, who grow old and fart and leave hairs all over the carpet, and then they say to their kids:

"Tarquin, don't crawl all over the dog hairs dear …"

And their living rooms have this stale omnipresent smell of damp dog, but they love their dogs and never appear to notice this subtle stench/aroma or the fact that their Hoover is so full of dog hair that it no longer "hoovers" up the usual detritus of everyday living – which continues to lie around the floor.

And their dogs bound up to me, a bit like Marmaduke, whenever I have the misfortune to pay a visit, and hardly let me get inside their front door before inspecting me in places that I had forgotten I have places and somehow putting their saliva all over my freshly pressed grey suit.

It is a picture of suburban hell. My friend is a young lady who lives with her husband and small daughter in a small flat in Kiev. She loves and adores her dogs; she even runs a small business making dog collars. How sweet. They only have one bedroom – which their little daughter uses. She and her husband make do with sleeping on the put-me-up sofa bed. The dogs sleep in the bathroom. Or in the hallway. In their house – the dogs get their morning bath before they bathe their little daughter. Something is wrong here in this order of life.

I, on the other hand – have always preferred cats. They do not get in your way. They do not need to go for walks, in the rain. They are their own masters. You can have a discussion with a cat. They don't say much, but when they have finished listening, either they agree with you and do whatever it is you wanted – or they don't. They just get up mid-sentence and go somewhere else.

Cats know when breakfast time is. They tell you. Life is a democracy, "Shall we have breakfast now?" They ask this politely at 06.30 enquiring from the foot of your bed. Just in case you didn't get the message, they gently wander up the duvet and gingerly reach out with one paw, claws extended, to touch your shoulder.

"Excuse me, but I just wanted to enquire … where is my breakfast?"

True, if it gets past this point, cats do become a little more aggressive. There is a tone of, "Miaaow …" which translates into;

"Look, I've been bloody reasonable, you know I have, but if I have to wait much longer, I will have to cannibalise my own body parts."

Of course, the cat doesn't actually say that; it's all in the inflection of the sound, and the look in their eyes.

And happy cats sleep. All the time. And they have this sort of contented smile and they purr when life is happy, and that makes you happy, too. They catch little animals, true, and it's not the fault of the animals, or of the cat – but you could say this is the natural order of things. So no, it's not the fault of the cat.

A dog, however, catches nothing. They sit and are obedient, or they knock small boys off bicycles. They do not have nine lives, and the only life they do have costs more than your private medical insurance in the vet's bills whenever anything goes wrong.

And yet as the years went by, I found myself being talked into this concept of "having a little dog" – as a companion.

"Richard, you know you would love someone to talk to…" goes the argument.

"Excuse me?"

Do I really look that stupid? Honest to God, I do know that the Rin Tin Tin and Lassie films and Disney films of talking dogs – are not real. There are no such things as talking dogs. Shrek and Spiderman are not real people. There is no such thing as Captain America, and neither true are those incredibly soppy movies about dogs who find their way home from the Antarctic back to Detroit. It is all a big lie, no doubt fostered by the food companies to encourage you and I to buy dog food, or buy into some notion that people do not need people. People need animals.

Now there is this psychological argument that in fact people do need cats, the single act of stroking a cat is remarkably relaxing; stress reducing goes the opinion. I can sort of buy into that.

But stroking dogs is another matter; for a start, they want you to do something and in fact you cannot escape from doing something; they sit there looking up at you, expectantly. It is a guilt trip.

I am sure the dog needs as much attention as we believe we need from them. It is a "giving" experience; and in my stressed life, as much as I would like to "give" more … I really do have other more deserving causes to give to. There is the Save the Antarctic fund, or the local Kids Home, or Keep My MP from Being Sacked fund, there are lots, all of them closer to my own needs and above all require absolutely nothing on my part other than giving a few quid by standing order. My conscience is clear, thank you very much.

But something was definitely missing, although I did not know it. And maybe that is the secret of love. When you find it, you know it. But you cannot go searching for it. Several young ladies I know tell me, they are "looking for a husband." They go to speed-dating nights; they sign up to internet matching. They get persuaded by "friends" to do blind dates.

"You know he is just your type; he can't help working for a Bank…" etc.

Yet they go to work with their headphones resolutely plugged into their ears, an iPad planted across their face, as if there was a sticker on their forehead saying "don't mess with me!"

If only they just chilled and looked around at life that was passing them by. The guy that happens to sit next to them on the tube. The man at the bus-stop who gets off at the wrong stop. It is being aware of these fleeting moments, that changes lives, where instinct and not reason, takes over.

And so, on a damp day last April, I am driving my Volvo to a place I have never visited, to see people I do not know, with money that I had earmarked for something else, to buy a little dog that I have never wanted.

You couldn't make it up.

Chapter Three

The Homecoming – Coming home; the rules of the game

In the same way as actually purchasing a car is not the issue – but actually 'owning and maintaining' it is the real event – so the slow dawn of this essential truth gradually hits me as I speed down the dual carriageway into suburban Plymouth, my little dog snuggled up between my legs in the driving seat. And so here we are, at my home, and now to be Home for Dog.

We have invested in a new bed for the dog. He will sleep in the utility room, next to the washing machine. He has his own litter pad. This is like some sort of Victorian servants' TV programme, where there is a definite division and social class. It will be some weeks before the little dog establishes his own credentials – or so we thought.

We have decided to call the dog – 'Barney'.

Barney the dog is a Westie crossed with a Cairn terrier. Even as a puppy, he has hair everywhere. Before you tell me that of course all dogs have hair everywhere – in his case, his hair grows over his eyes, over his mouth, it is scruffy even after being combed and he has that look of having just got up – all the time. He is a dishevelled scrap with his own distinct personality and character. He has the most inquisitive nature of anything I have ever seen. He wants to KNOW. He learns very quickly. He has a loving nature that believes everyone must be his friend – until proven otherwise. And even then, he is prepared to give you at least a couple of chances.

This latter quality is very useful when meeting the cat.

The cat was concerned, but not worried. Almost tolerant when it became clear (to the cat) that the feeding area for both animals would be the same. After all, we cannot feed one pet in say the living room, and the other in the utility area. But clearly Barney would have to learn that the cat has his own food, and his own space.

Personal space is important for cats. For Barney, his first real lesson in life was when he bounced up to the cat, tried to sniff his nether parts, and was met by a casual slap by the cat who had turned round and just nonchalantly waved one paw, claws extended, in Barney's face.

And thus the pecking order of supremacy was established. Adults might or might not have breakfast first. But either way, doggy was definitely last in the order of the human race. This was to become a life-defining situation, to which Barney has yet to find an answer, and certainly did not have life's skills to deal with it when it (literally) hit him in the face. We had thought the relationship would at some point metamorphose into something like the give and take of two guys living with each other in a rented flat. Similar to Jack Lemon and Walther Matthau in *The Odd Couple*. Alas no – it's never got beyond, to this day, the dog being terrified whenever the cat decides to block his path, or become supremely jealous when the cat is stroked … but not him. Barney would hide behind my legs when watching TV if the cat decided to wander in and plonk himself down next to the remote.

But not every day was about learning to live with a cat, and in the same way as there is always "somebody' in the office that you and I will never get on with, however hard we try – so began a learning curve of how to handle life's rules and regulations and yet carve out your own identity and set of rules that the rest of the house in their turn, must abide from you.

First of these, is that, if I let you stroke my head, then I will roll over and allow you to rub my tummy. I will be available for this process at any time of the day, whenever we meet. I will give you licks every morning because I love you very much – but only on condition that I lick the dinner plates when you have finished eating (see Chapter 2) – after all, fair's fair, isn't it? I understand that you have to de-flea me every now and then, and privately speaking, the little comb you use actually feels quite good, so it's no great hardship. I will do my best to stay in the garden and only run down the bank, across the neighbour's lawn and into the deep undergrowth beyond – if I see a fox somewhere or there are some pigeons that are annoying me.

Unfortunately, Barney's sense of reasonable compromise, at just a couple of months old, did not pass the test of community living. Twice in the first two weeks, I got a call from someone who I never knew lived just a few doors down the road:

"Do you have a little dog?"

The concept of social compromise, of saying what is right for the situation, whether it is true or not, is best seen when you grovel to your neighbour. Apparently half of all legal disputes are now between once friendly neighbours, and I can see why:

"Oh, I'm *so* sorry! Did he really destroy your entire new flowerbed?"

"No, it's fine, really – I'll just have to get the new gardener back from his day job at Kew Gardens, to replant. He's such a lovely little puppy, isn't he?"

The first night at home, is not good. It is not that Barney does not understand the concept of sleep-time. It is that he is crying. This is not pleasant to hear. These are not angry tears of the sort "You know I wanted to go out with my friends but you have stopped me!" These are sobs. I am truly loath to carry Barney to my bedroom so he can sleep there. So I sit by little Barney, while he finally, and what seems like hours and hours later – finally drifts off to sleep. I, too, am already near to the point of clinical sleep deprivation. I am sure the people at Guantanamo would do far better just getting each inmate to look after a puppy. There is only so long that your social conscience and human endurance can handle this.

What is surprising in this process – is that little Barney gets through this early homecoming stage – in just a week or two. True, I was not expecting it to be all plain sailing and he would chip in and start doing the laundry or the supermarket run in just a few days. I did expect there to be a day or two of adjustment, i.e., probably a month or probably never. Actually I had no idea.

But when after just a few nights I found I could snuggle the little animal in his bed and he knew what the deal was, and happily he curled up and went to sleep with his selection of little toys and other squeaky things that he played with – in bed with him – and I too could take a glass of Baileys, catch the evening football, and then go to bed myself. Then suddenly it dawned on me that Barney was now Family. He was not some sort of addition that I had bought from Currys or the PC Shop, to go with my Wi-Fi. This was a real, living, thing, that had thoughts and a will of his own, however embryonic. In short, I could not take him back.

I now understood why they don't do Gift Receipts for little animals. Once you get past the first couple of days, then you are lost, the game is over. Doggy has adopted you. You now have this absolute obligation that pees and poos, that munches lumps out of your sofa and that uses your grand piano legs as a scratching post.

But what is bizarre is – none of this seems to matter. My grand piano is my most treasured possession but here I am nonchalantly picking up the yellow pages to call the furniture restorer:

"Yep, do you polish out deep scratches on furniture? You do? Only £250.00 plus VAT. Yes of course, tomorrow is fine…"

As I write this, there is a tradesman in Plymouth who is already on the phone to Virgin Atlantic to book his summer vacation to Miami. There is this complete lack of financial common sense when it comes to pet management, similar to parents who only have one child, or who put their kids through private school – ostensibly to get the "education" they never had.

"Yes of course he must have a Ken Barrington signed original Cricket Bat, if that's what the School says he must have!"

Apparently you can get Swarovski implanted dog collars, which I am sure are very cool, etc. – but my point is – the little dog will not be that bothered either way. He will not know that his dog collar comes from the cheapest supermarket, or from the designer shops in Bond Street, London. As far as I am aware, dogs are not brand savvy. It is simply that as people, WE alas, are. Walking through a five-star hotel in Nice a few years ago, the maître d' offered the young lady a glass of champagne for breakfast, and enquired if her pet pooch, who obediently trailed behind – also would want to take one.

Barney in fact does not want a dog collar at all. He gives me a look similar to Morgan Freedman in the Shawshank Redemption when he is chained up, and I feel bad about explaining that this device is for his own good. Yes it will stop him running under traffic, but the reality is that it will also stop him from running into next door's garden.

It will take some months before Barney understands the concept of English property law and trespass, as the only words he currently understands are; "Barney, dinner!" and "Sit!"

This is very much one paw forward and one paw back.

Of all my misconceptions – I think the greatest was that the little dog would be completely lost in his new surroundings, like a new born babe and that we, as "parents" would have to feed and monitor and bathe and do the baby things for several months. It is now exactly 11 months on since that fateful day last year, and Barney is still a little uncontrollable kid when you mention the word "Walkies". And in the same way that a mother will always recognize her own baby crying amongst a room full of little howling kids – so it became obvious when Barney barks from half way down the garden – that this is completely ear piercing and tuned into my own personal psyche that other dogs simply had not breached.

I was amazed how quickly Barney adjusted to every room in the house. He found that as soon as he could find a way to jump up onto the bed – then "every" bed became "his" bed. He would sleep sitting next to whoever was in bed, whether they were listening to Radio 5 Live, or iTunes rock. Little dog was not so much a party animal – but definitely a social animal. The Homecoming had metamorphosed in a matter of days into the Adoption.

And so begins the process of customization. Does Barney have an Arsenal dog collar – or a Chelsea one? Does he wait until all the household have got up before going for a pee in the morning? Or does he get let out to roam the garden, bark at the birds in the trees, annoy the neighbours at 7.00 in the morning – and for how long does the magic shout of "chewstick!" work until he realizes that this is a subtle and devious way to get him back inside? It is a learning curve, for me as a parent so to say – and the dog as a terrible twos little kid.

But what is the most interesting is that at no time does the love affair ever fade. It is not like, OK – I have had him for a few weeks and months – guys, it was fun – but – you know enough is enough. It's work time, I really do have to go to the office … sort of plan. And even the cat and the dog are talking to each other. This is against all natural laws of relationships, and I am sitting on my sofa and the dog is jumping up on one side and the cat is asleep on the other, and I am thinking – for heaven's sake, what do I do if I need to get the remote to watch the football?

Somehow, having a little dog creates a new level of decision making and compromises. But maybe this is what life is about. Have dog – be good to humanity. Sounds like a plan.

Chapter Four

The Cat – Learning life's valuable lesson that the cat comes first

"There is something about a dog crying, that is not nice to hear…"

This was not the first time the cat had seen-off an intruder, an interloper into his space, so to say. Boh – the cat – knew about interlopers and invasions of space. He had seen off several rabbits, proudly brought in several little, mice, birds and several squirrels from the garden until even this pastime began to bore him, and he'd eaten the pet hamster.

The pet hamster, named Fergus – was probably the cruelest. He had been caught early on in his life when the cat had pushed his cage onto the floor, worked out how to open the door, and then caught the little animal as he tried to scurry away. But God was smiling on Fergus that day. We managed to save the poor thing and, by positioning his rear legs inside a toilet roll and giving him something to hold onto with his front paws – we fed him milk and nuts from a pair of tweezers – and gradually he built up his strength and little Fergus learned to walk again.

He never forgot that instance, and was always wary of the cat.

Alas, it was I that had become complacent. Some months later opening the garden door to the cat who wanted to come in – I completely forgot that Fergus was asleep on the arm of the sofa.

It was over in seconds – and this time there was no miracle revival, no stroking of his chest, and no kiss of life. Hamster was no more, and something went missing in my own life from that moment on.

So the arrival of Barney, in theory, did not anticipate much trepidation in my eyes, except that I had forgotten one thing. Dogs grow to be bigger than cats and this, as I found out, manifests itself into a subtle change of relationship between said dog and cat, where a mutual tolerance of existence slowly and gradually develops.

But as much as Barney is an unconditional love machine – so Boh is a "love me on my terms" social animal.

"You want to lick my balls, huh? (Apart from the fact that I don't have any) – well, tell me, just what do I get out of this, my friend?"

And on my terms – it certainly started to be. I gently held the little puppy in my arms and introduced him to the cat. For Barney – this was Friend! Someone more or less the same size as him, although slightly bigger, but certainly not human. So it was someone he could communicate with. At least worth a try. Barney wagged his tail and made to inspect the cat's nether regions. Boh the cat was having none of this, and promptly turned round and gave Barney a clout with his front paw. Barney went tearfully to my legs not comprehending this reaction, and the cat just looked on as if to say – "There's an order of servitude in this place, mate, and that means I get my neck stroked first and I also get my breakfast first, and I get the best bed."

You can learn a lot from physical violence. Just one swipe establishes a complete behaviour pattern, it sets some ground rules.

But little Barney was nothing if not persistent. It is one thing hiding behind Mum's legs when attacked by wolfhounds in the park (see here and later chapters) – completely different when being attacked by something not much bigger than you and in YOUR own territory.

So the chess game continued, with Barney learning to choose his moments when he offered the paw of friendship, and the cat gradually softening his stance.

For the cat, too, this was a learning experience. Here was a little animal that was not protected in a metal cage, that was by this time growing to be same size as him. He could push Barney around in a strategic sort of way – but the tactics had to change. Giving clouts round the ear just did not cut it anymore. There had to be other more subtle ways.

Best of all was going to sleep in Barney's bed. There is forbidden territory, and forbidden territory, and one's bed has to be high up on the ranking of places that are No Go areas and Barney did not know how to handle this. Instead of getting annoyed, he decided to get a second opinion, i.e., looking at me with that look of disgust that says – "Can you see what he is doing!?" "And are you not going to do something about it?"

Body language is a great communicator. And yet slowly, surely, over the first nine months, both sides started to accept that maybe there could be same sort of mutual existence. And it was nice to see – a sort of humanization of a relationship. The cat learned some tricks from Barney – how to sneak food from dining plates, how to look cute and get treats. Up until then, the cat had just assumed that food would come when he bawled and asked for it, and up to that point, that was how life was. Now suddenly, there was a new order of life that required a new set of life skills.

As time went on, the dog became remarkably good at protecting the family. No more could the cat pinch the sausages that were lying open to defrost. A sudden outburst of barking was a wake up call, that we soon learnt meant; "The Cat is nicking the lunch". A soft growl meant that the birds in the garden were invading his space. I had to remind Barney that this was not a Hitchcock movie. Birds did not mean a violent and savage death. And similarly, dogs and cats on the TV were simply that – they were on TV. Trying to get Barney to understand that TV was not real was a lesson in communicative discussion.

What to say? As much as this has been about a small dog learning to live with his new surroundings – so this was a lesson of a cat doing the same, at a level that he had previously not encountered. This was a greater human experience that mirrored society as a whole, a sort of 'arranged marriage' to see how two people can somehow forge a friendship despite all inherent suspicions and reservations.

Chapter Five

The Neighbours – You may covet your neighbour's garden, but you may not run around in it

Westies are protective animals. They are hunters and gatherers. Small as they are, nobody messes with a Westie. Little Barney knew that from his first day at his new home. Nobody told him to bark at the birds. He just knew.

Once a few weeks had passed and he was allowed out into the garden, then the rights of ownership prevailed. This was HIS garden. Whatever deal had been done with voles, other cats, birds and squirrels before – these were last century. There was a new order, a new structure.

Unfortunately, nobody told Barney that the hedge and brambles at the bottom of the garden meant that – beyond that – the garden belonged to someone else.

It was similar to several years ago when my daughter had a pet rabbit that escaped and ate all of my neighbour's expensive and freshly planted flowers. Even the United Nations and the Archangel Gabriel could not have had the diplomatic skills to sort that one out. I overheard my neighbour saying he would use his gun and shoot the rabbit.

No, this needed to be sorted, and quickly, otherwise we would have no neighbours left. Yet there was no easy answer – at least there did not seem to be early in the morning. For a start, there was no point in keeping the little dog indoors, because at that time, he was already desperate to go to the toilet, and had already peed, etc., on the floor in the utility area where he had his bed.

I, too, was getting totally pissed myself having to clean up this, every time I made the early morning tea.

No – the answer had to be to let him out, let him do his ritual barking – but somehow teach him that there were real benefits in not jumping the neighbour's wall and invading their space.

The answer – when it finally dawned on me – was in the classic male attitude that you get to a man's heart, through his stomach. The magic words "Barney, Breakfast!" – Had much more appeal with the certainty of food – than any notional exploration and protection of property. And so it began; a ritual morning activity where; 1) dog would be let out; 2) – he would scamper round the garden doing whatever it is that dogs do at that time in the morning; and 3) hurry back to make sure the cat had not eaten his breakfast.

And it worked every time. No more pee in the utility area, happy neighbours, and also happy birds. As soon as Barney had finished his ritual walkabout, etc. – so the birds would then appear and bathe in the birdbath, look for food, tweet about – all safe in the knowledge that Barney was engrossed elsewhere.

There were advantages for Barney in this process too. It meant that – if I left the kitchen door open – he could charge upstairs after eating, and jump on our bed, and give a welcome kiss, full of love and appreciation. Only dogs can do this with this level of devotion. A colleague of mine in Oslo said to me recently that, "The best way to recover from a bad day at work – is to go home – then walk out of the door – and then immediately come in again. Your dog will welcome you home the first time – and then also welcome you home the second time, with equal love and unconditional affection, whether you have been away for half a day or half a minute."

So true.

But while this process works within the confines of one's own garden – a different set of exponential rules apply when going walkies and charging into other peoples' gardens that are further down the road – or next to the Park – or anywhere that is away from home.

For Barney – there is no logical distinction between someone else's garden, and his own. The equation goes something like; "If I love you, then why should you not love me?" The concept of unrequited love is not yet fully formed, and will only be learnt by frequent bellowing of that immortal phrase, "Barney – Bad Dog!"

"Bad Dog" does indeed mean something. Barney's ears drop down, he looks sullen, he walks dolefully to his bed … but these actions are after the event. This does not help when Barney escapes his lead, charges into a garden somewhere up our road, makes friends with some local builders who are doing some work, and promptly starts running around someone else's flower bed. This time there was no forgiveness. The woman opened her window and shouted, "Get that dog out of here!" There was also the invitation to come meet her husband. I demurred at that invitation, but catching Barney was not easy. This was game time. Even though he knew he was doing wrong, this situation was still fun time cum laude.

But I was increasingly worried. For a start, this was an expensive house and garden, and they had an expensive Land Rover Disco in the drive. People that have that sort of money know how to protect it, and I did not fancy a lawsuit at 8.00 in the morning. Equally, the woman shouting at me through her window was in no mood to have a genteel philosophical discussion about the finer points of dog handling. It's not often that I hear profane language from a woman at any time, let alone when I am starting my day. After several seconds but what seemed like half a year – I finally trapped Barney, picked him up and carried him the hundred yards back home and his utility area.

This was a lesson in life. A bit like going to church. There was this vicar I knew who was asked to preach for two weeks running, at my local church. He preached the same sermon – on Sin – each time. When questioned about this afterwards, he said simply – "Well, I repeated it, because I can see you weren't listening the first time."

I learnt that neighbours cannot be judged by their surroundings, or what they say in public. The reality check for neighbours is; "If thou lovest my dog, then stop giving him a hard time, and let him give you a lick."

Chapter Six

Walkies – Who is taking whom for a walk?

I always knew that part of the deal with owning a dog – was the ritual of Walkies. What I didn't know was that Westies are not stupid animals. It had also never dawned on me that the word "walks" or "walk-around" – or any collection of words that included the word "walk" – would be the Get Up And Go trigger for Barney to come bounding along, dog lead in his mouth, tail wagging furiously, and plonk himself in front of me.

And it was not only my voice, or my family's voices, that provoked this response. Any TV channel that featured a barking dog, a soppy Disney movie about/ dogs that could talk, or even any Rom Com movie where the guy asks the girl to "walk home" ... was a sort of Pavlov dog reaction of; ears up, looking around, with a sort of question that said, "Did I REALLY hear the W word?"

And there we were in this desperate cycle of behaviour, that when ending in disappointment, Barney would offer a small "humph", flopping down on the carpet, and having a play with his toy squeaky bone that almost became a lament.

At first, walkies were an adventure for both of us. I found myself in a vortex of life and people and civilization that had hitherto passed me. People with Dogs were like an alien species. They were everywhere. Everybody had a little pooch that they were dragging along behind them to the park – or the dogs were dragging the humans behind them – but it was like the Invasion of the Body Snatchers, or the later Stepford Wives. Everyone was mindlessly, but resolutely walking along, letting their chosen animal off their respective leads, chatting to everyone else in the local park – whose names they all knew. And not just the humans' names. Everyone knew all the dogs' names as well.

So you would have conversations like this:

"And how is Minnie?" I would ask.

"Oh she's fine now … she had a lovely facial last week."

"Excuse me?"

"Yes; my daughter Minnie. OH! You meant Jessie, the Labradoodle," etc.

I used to marvel at the wonderful existence of these women who had nothing more to do in life than engage in banal conversation. The women themselves were in deep conversation about supermarket visits and cooking tonight. It was in some ways scary and in other ways an eye opener. Having a dog was the best pulling mechanism known to man. I could engage happily in equally banal conversation, impress all with my 'touchy feely' side, empathize with their difficulties. All I needed to do was close the deal:

"Shall we take a coffee? My place is nearby?"

The only problem alas was the dog. I could hardly leave him behind while I tried to pull the owner of Barney's own paramour.

"Yep, Barney – you keep running around, there's a good boy! I'll only be a few minutes!" Well, maybe more than a few minutes, but what was the key catalyst to getting in front of these 20 year old – 35 year old attractive ladies – was at the same time the key obstacle to progressing further.

It reminded me of my student days at Uni, where the ratio of women to men was 10 – 1. It was like that Hugh Grant movie of a similar name, where the guy works out the secret of eternal life is, how to get alongside single mums who need adult male attention.

The only other guy to walk his dog at the same time as me was an OAP who used to go walkies for himself so he could have a ciggy on the seats in the park while his dog bounded off and terrorized all the other dogs. I never saw him get up and chase after his dog or try to engage in dialogue with anybody. He wheezed a lot, his back was a bit hunched – and in my more unsympathetic moments – which were many – I just prayed to God to say, "Please don't let me end up like that!" As a friend of mine used to say – life is too short to drink cheap wine.

He controlled his dog by having some sort of electric remote tagging thing on the dog collar. It actually gave a sort of electric shock. The dog would suddenly arch backwards, and then run back to his master. I am sure these things are not legal, and whilst part of me wanted to interfere and say to the older guy, "look, I don't want to be rude" – (actually I didn't mind being rude, but you know how these conversations go?) – "but I don't think your dog should be doing this," but I really did not want to get involved with the guy's dog, who was terrorizing all the other dogs and had alas a penchant for trying to 'mount' my Barney.

Barney did not want at all to be mounted. He was doing his best to run back to hide behind my own legs. But he, on the other hand was happily trying to chat up little Rosie, the cock-a-poo who was also in the park and his sort of 'girlfriend', if dogs have 'girlfriends'. So you had this mélange of conflicting interests, each resulting in a level of hesitation that solved nothing and made me more and more tense.

Walkies were just not fun anymore.

Clearly something had to be done, – but the question was – what? The answer presented itself the very next day. When a man's got to do, etc. The next morning, when this ritual was about to be played out, yet again, and the old guy was sitting there, tobacco aroma as usual, his dog trying to climb on top of Barney and take a lump out of his neck. I made my approach.

Maybe I was a bit too blunt. Maybe commercial life was interfering in my sense of human values. The older man looked up, with surprise and sadness in his eyes, and a look of sorrow.

"But my dog loves your dog. He does not like the others. Your dog is so friendly. He has no one else to play with."

OMG.

I just wished the ground would open up and whisk me away or wind the clock back to yesterday or do something – but not this. I was hoping God, who had now clearly deserted me in my hour of need, would come down with his flock of angels and rescue either me, or the old man, and take his dog to nirvana, or wherever God takes reluctant dogs and their owners. I mumbled a few words. Life had not prepared me for this. Yes, it's true, there are moments when just at the wrong time, I open my big mouth and say something just a little sharp, and instantly regret it, usually to family, and then after an hour, I return and apologise. We all do it. That does not make me feel much better and it doesn't absolve me of guilt, but it's one thing having a sharp word with your wife/partner/husband about "for heaven's sake, just how many times do I have to ask you to put the bins out?!" – And this single moment where one inconsiderate statement, without knowledge of the deeper situation – can wound a person who may have nothing left. And I had just taken away his one moment of happiness, seeing his dog play with mine.

The older man called his dog – or at least pressed his remote toy, and his dog, duly arched back – stood still for a moment – and then came running up. He was not a big dog, but bigger than Barney. I stood still. I had no words at all for this, and watched as the man slowly shuffled away and his dog followed him.

The usual crowd of attractive women in the park was nowhere to be seen.

Yet walks became an attraction for me, too, in other ways. Barney clearly relished the "me – time". This was his moment for bonding with Dad. We had conversations. We developed a routine. The church lawn became a good place for doing little pees and the neighbour with the white wall was the chosen spot for doing a poo. It was as if there was some God given order in the world; as if God had smiled on his young offspring and It Was Good.

It was as if there was a real communication going on – Barney would flop around the house, with that "humph" of a noise if "walkies time" came and went, and yet would understand if I sat down with him and said, "Look, Dad has got a problem, OK? I need a few more minutes." It once again reminded me of Jack Lemmon and Walter Matthau in *The Odd Couple* having this eternal domestic compromise of what are we going to do next?

Barney was getting into a routine. He liked the predictability of it all. There was waking up in the morning, breakfast with the cat, run upstairs to wake my wife up, and either get me off to work, or do walkies. He knew what to expect. His little tail would go so fast it would power the hydroelectric pumps in the local river. Walkies meant happiness. Didn't they? Barney's mouth would crease up at the corners into what could only be a smile. Maybe God had rescued us after all.

Chapter Seven

The Wolfhound – Not every dog is smaller than you; some are a lot bigger!

Let's try to put this into a human life experience. What happens when your son/daughter starts going out with, has a relationship with – someone you know who is totally unsuitable? Someone that you know, as a person of experience – will never be able to make it work out.

The sudden understanding that all dogs are not "dog-sized", and that some are the size of fully grown donkeys – is one of those lessons in doggie life similar to 'not all companies are the same'. Some are employee friendly, some are honest, and most are not, etc.

Wolfhounds are seriously lovable and seriously large. Seeing the arrival of Barney, who was a new kid on the block, demanded some serious investigation, definitely some running around, and boy – we can have a real little frisky fun here!

Joining in the running around, Barney soon found himself on the wrong end of the game – being chased by not one but two large wolfhounds, who – in their defence – were simply having fun.

But having fun was not Barney's interpretation of one large dog sitting on you or fighting you – however playfully. Barney would come running back, yelping, hiding behind my legs.

"Look what they've done to me! Shouldn't you be doing something about this? Are there not laws? Can we not phone someone?"

Gradually, Barney managed to work out that, taking things slowly and softly, was the way out of this mess. It took some time to register. Days and weeks went by, each time my dreading arriving at the local park, to see the arrival of the dog owner and his two enormous hounds The problem is that, for owners who have large dogs, they see their animals as 'gentle giants'.

"Oh, you mean Oscar? Isn't he such a lovable big bear?"

Er … well, actually – no he isn't. And he's molesting my little dog who is only a month or two old and is blatantly terrified. There seems to be an unwritten law in the universe of human relationships, akin to; "I can criticize my mother … but you must never criticize your mother-in-law," type of thing.

So you have to play the game, go along for the ride.

"Why yes! Isn't he just … adorable! But… would you mind asking him to stop beating the hell out of my own little pooch who is too terrified to run away?"

There are some things you can say in life – and others you can't. It is not quite at the level of Creon and Antigone in their discussion on the need for social hypocrisy, but what it does is force you to come up with tangential ways around the problem.

For Barney – his answer was that love is the best form of defence. That small size can be an advantage when the larger animal is not asking for a fight, just asking for some sort of interaction. Barney wandered up to the Wolfhound and muzzled up and gave him big lick. A sort of bromance. Sure I may be smaller, but we are buddies, right?

In business, one of the best ways to win a discussion, – is to apologise first.

"Look – let me apologise – you are so right/insightful/strategic – (Please delete which adjective does not work for you) – I was just thinking that … blah, blah, blah…"

This of course elicits the response;

"Why no! I was out of order! I was reflecting that your ideas do indeed have some merit …" and on it goes. You can't fight someone who apologizes.

And so it became for Barney, keep your friends close – but your enemies closer. People pay money for Management Textbooks and attend expensive consulting courses to find out this stuff. How naive! The answer is right in front of you, just watching two dogs, working out their relationships, through interaction in the local park.

Chapter Eight

The Bath – Yes it's like having your own spa

One of the signs of someone growing up – is the increase of personal body odour around them. We have ways of combating this. We all spend vast amounts of cash on this or that deodorant that does or does not leave a white stain; or we get seduced by branding and we are into Tom Ford, or we buy into whichever famous actor or actress image that says by implication, that we are as cool, as attractive, as successful – as the label on the bottle of whatever it is of which we have just spent large amounts of money.

And in many ways this is not our fault. We are victims of marketing of necessity. Walk into any young male teenager's bedroom, and the aroma of stale sweat hits you before you even make it over the threshold. It's a rite of passage. Maybe it's a hormonal thing; perhaps it is. As we become more and more aware of our need for relationships, and the changes that are happening to us – so we start growing up, so to say, and the act of taking a bath takes on a new significance, it is a relaxation, we put out some scented candles, it is a Zen experience, similar to those Spa experiences, where we match up our Ying and Yang, or whatever it is we do. I go to my local Spa every now and then. There is this music that sounds like a sort of strangled budgie and I get transported into this nirvana of happiness and deep chill, while I am trying to make out the chord progressions of the strange music.

Sure, we have had baths before. Our parents bathed us. We know what they are. They have been fun. We would play with our rubber ducks. If there was ever a sign that humans started life in some sort of embryonic form in water – then our love for A BATH surely takes the biscuit.

Unfortunately, dogs do not see it that way.

For Barney, having a bath, does not make him more attractive to Rosie, the little cock-a-poo cross breed that follows him everywhere. It also makes no difference to young Jessie as he chases her round in circles in the park, whether he has a subtle Aramis aroma, or not. He simply wants to smell her rear-parts; and she is happy enough to let him.

If beauty is in the eye of the beholder, Barney is becoming a handsome and cool little dog with a maturity beyond his years. His mangey look of tousled hair gives him a sort of unkempt appearance, in the same way that teenage girls can look great even if they just wear a bin-liner, because their physique is what it takes.

So for Barney, this is not a romantic or somehow pleasurable experience. The need for a bath, is quite simply because, after three months of human living-Barney is beginning to smell. Cuddles with Barney are becoming an unpleasant experience. He rushes up to see me every evening when I come home, but my welcome is tempered by, "Whoa, hang on while I change out of my suit."

Barney's first bath – is an experience of persuasion and mistrust. He knows what a bath as such is, i.e., he knows that adults go there and they get covered in water. He knows that adults seem to like this experience, but getting into a deep pool of clean water where you could conceivably die – for no reason whatsoever – is not his idea of fun.

The fact is – Barney does not like water (although he will make an exception for muddy puddles). He does not like stepping out into the rain. He would rather cross his legs and suffer than run out into the rain to do a pee in the garden. He insists we take an umbrella if we go for a walkies in the rain. This is ridiculous; he is a dog for God's sake.

He follows me upstairs; the girl at Pets At Home assures me that this doggie shampoo really is the business … I am not quite sure how she knows, but I let this question pass. Somehow – maybe from the inflection in my voice. Barney knows that this time when I say; "Barney, chewsticks!" – He knows, he just knows that there are no chewsticks. It is a lesson in deception. Westies may look cute, but they are not stupid. Deception only happens once … Next time, we will have to think of a better argument.

It is redolent of Barney's infrequent visits to the Vet – his little legs start shaking even before we stop the car and there is this "look" as he stares up from the back seat of the car, "I don't want to go in there!"

So we have this stand-off. Worse, Barney is getting stronger. He is no longer a puppy. It takes two adults to persuade him a) to get in the bath in the first place; and b) one to hold him and one to administer the shampoo, the shower, the drying afterwards.

This stand-off is going nowhere. I pick up Barney, and he is BIG. He weighs a ton. I had forgotten how heavy he is becoming. Perhaps this is what Rosie sees in him. I am just so grateful that he does not bear grudges. My ex-wife used to bear grudges and look where that got us …

I gently deposit him in the bathtub and my wife starts showering him with tepid water. He looks miserable, I look desperate – and I am saying ridiculous things like;

"Hey, little guy" (I never call anybody 'little guy') – "you're going to look great!" And so on.

Barney does not look great. I have never seen him so resigned, as if his faith in human nature has just been evaporated. The people he trusted! How could they?

The water, however, is deep black. Barney is filthy. His multi layers of hair keep producing a residue of brown and black and dirty water that takes forever to run clear and clean.

I am shocked, in fact. I look at my wife. "How did he get as dirty as THIS?" She responds with:

"Well, this is what dogs do. They get dirty!"

In fact, Barney is becoming fastidious about his personal cleanliness. He does wash himself, he inspects himself, he knows when things are not right – within him – and my criticism is unfair.

Eventually we take Barney down to the living room in front of the fire and spread a towel across the floor. He shakes himself, and he rolls around and over and over until he gets dry.

But the whole episode is a realization that we are not dealing with a dog here, any more. This is the same growth path of having kids, the honeymoon period, the coochy coochy coos of the first few months and then the hard slog forever, of bringing them up in a democratic environment where I am the only one with a vote.

Except that Barney wants a vote too. The "humph" of resignation as he slumps on the living room floor, is different from the yelps of delight or terror at the park. The barking when he sees birds in the garden is different from the morning conversation with the Border Collie just a few doors down the road, a lovely young lady dog called Lily, who once escaped and came round to see Barney.

Dogs are as enlightened as we are, and it's as if female dogs have no problem wandering up my garden and sort of arriving at the back door: "Can Barney play today?" In the same way my cat seems to think that we are just bigger cats, and frankly we are lucky he is around and how can it possibly be that we do not understand when he wants feeding? Barney and the way we communicate with him, is becoming almost human.

I am beginning to understand the subtle language difference of each statement of intent from Barney, each tilt of his head, the ears up or down.

My wife once caught me at my local train station, where she and Barney came to see me off one morning, actually bending down to have a deep conversation about the 7.47 a.m. from Plymouth to London, and it was a big train, and …

"Richard," she quietly said, "you are looking stupid."

But that'so the issue. It did not feel stupid. If Barney is supposed to be "my best friend" then am I not his best friend, too? Of course not. He is a dog. He has his doggy friends and I have my wife and family etc., and we all come together at various times, and we all get on in harmony. Except at bath times.

Chapter Nine

The Sea – A bigger bath and much colder

We live in a women's world. Whatever people say about Glass Ceilings, and Superwomen, and Leaning In, or Leaning Out, there is a plausible argument along the lines of "women actually are in control" of their own destiny. They know what works for them.

The obvious discussion is that women can "choose" when to have children, or whether not to, and how to balance that with a lifestyle and income choice.

Clearly it's a discussion topic. It's provocative – but it overlooks the basic evidence that Men, on the other hand – don't have those realistic lifestyle options.

Sure, in these days of homeworking, of remote Skype based meetings, of touchy feely New Men, we can argue that the boundaries are blurred and for some indeed they are. But generally speaking, just looking at the thousands of faceless men who cross the London Bridge every morning as they walk up to Bank tube station to work, it is men who are seen as hunters. The first question that two men will always ask each other on first meeting will be; "And what do you do?"

It is never – "And how are the kids?" – men are defined by their work in life, and not by their situation in their family. Men are, or were, supposed to be – Real Men.

Real Men do things like; put up shelves, cut down trees and go to the pub with their mates.

All of which is a problem, if you don't conform to that stereotype.

And which is a problem if you are a little dog – who does not like getting his feet wet when running along the nearby beach, and when all his friends are splashing about in the sea alongside.

So; here we are. Today we are going to the seaside. The beach is only a couple of minutes away by car. Barney knows about cars. He sees himself as the co-driver, jumps up into the passenger seat of my wife's sporty low-hung DS3, settles down, and waits for me to fasten his seat belt. Barney is already heavy enough to register when he is sitting there, and the car makes an irritating ringing noise if I can't be bothered to fix the

55

belt. I don't know why I bother at all. Barney moves over slips out of the seat belt and puts his paws up on the window.

We take the back streets, and soon find the suburban road out to the beach. The road narrows as we climb up the unmade road to the car park – and we park up, with a most fantastic view of the Plymouth estuary below, and the sandy beach, beneath.

Barney is beside himself. I let him off his lead and he scuttles down the steps, promptly races across the sand to play with another little dog who is primly sitting next to her rather genteel owners.

This is like that scene in *The Aristocats*, Barney playing the part of the Alley Cat that wins the girl in the end. Except that whilst the young female dog here in question is giving all the right buying signals, alas the family adjacent have no wish for their new Sloane wellington boots to be splashed by a local west country piece of rough.

The family make a move for higher ground, I catch up with Barney, and we gently explore the rocks and pools of water that contain crabs and probably effluent. I'm sure this is one of the beaches where South West Water has a safety warning,

Or maybe not. There are some people in wetsuits professionally starting to do surfing on bodyboards out in the small waves, and I am trying to encourage Barney to venture into the water proper – do more than just run through the stream that gives out into the sea, or the small ends of waves that finally drag themselves up into the beach itself. Surely it's time for Barney to learn to swim?

This seems a reasonable enough idea to me. Whenever there are stories in the media of dogs falling into difficulty in a rough river or frozen lake, etc. – it is always the dogs who somehow manages to survive and find a way out, and the idiot humans who jump in and try to rescue them – promptly drown.

I am not saying that this solution is reasonable; I am saying that there has to be something hard-wired into every dog that tells them how to survive in water.

Unfortunately, God seems to have forgotten to upload the latest software upgrade for Barney. I throw his favourite squeaky red rubber bone into the sea; Barney makes a move into the water, then stops and turns and looks at me with a look that says:

"Are you bloody joking?! Do you know I could possibly drown out there?!"

Barney runs back to me, sits between my legs, and makes a sort of high-pitched whining noise, which loosely translated, means:

"This is my favourite bone … and it is floating away … and you threw it there … and I will love you forever if you wouldn't't mind stepping in up to your waist to rescue my little toy…" This is a sort of moral blackmail, and I have no answer and frankly no choice.

One thing is for sure. I cannot go home without the little squeaky red bone. I had a fleeting thought that I could pass by Pets At Home and get a replacement (a replacement bone … not dog) – I mean my wife will never know – but that thought was dismissed as quickly as it arrived.

No. Now is the time to be a Real Man. An action-hero. But what to do about the dog? I can hardly leave him there just sitting on the sand, while his master wades off into the sunset, in true John Wayne style, "I've come for my Boy" type of macho movie. Hollywood is full of this sort of "I'm going to a Better Place" type of movies, and I suppose this is where most men get their guilt trip. Aren't we supposed to be like that, – putting ourselves second, and so forth, for the greater good?

I pick up Barney, who is not comfortable and neither am I. I start to walk into the small waves, and out into the slightly deeper water, where the squeaky little red bone is still floating around. The water is already way higher than my wellington boots, but I have long ago given up thinking I will stay dry for this little experimental day together.

Bundling Barney under one arm – I reach down, pick out the little toy – and triumphant – I splash back to the safety of dry land, or at least solid ground. I plonk Barney down on the sand, attach his lead, and we gingerly retrace our footsteps up to the car park above. This has clearly not been the greatest idea of my life.

But then again – maybe it has?

What are we expecting out of this? Obviously Barney is going to be excited, phased, not sure of the rules of the game – because there are no rules of the game. As far as he is concerned, he is in as much deep water as I am in terms of what actually do you do, what is expected of him? After all, he is not Lassie or Rin Tin Tin – swimming out to save the confederates from disaster across the river torrent in Tennessee or somewhere.

And finally – when we get back to the car – Barney is a happy little guy. I wrap the towel around him, dry his paws, and he jumps into the front passenger seat of the car. I am sure it will not be long before he jumps into the driver's side and starts to look for the keys. Maybe beach-time is about male bonding.

Barefoot, I slide into the driver's seat, turn on the heater, and – back in my own comfort zone, speed up the hill and back to civilization.

Chapter Ten

Life – How to learn that not all neighbours are your friends

Time marches on. Maybe it marches quicker as we get older. I always remember that yearning when I was at junior school that my birthday was SOOOO far away, next week even. The days lasted for ever, and a year – well, I could not contemplate a year. In those days, my definition of old age was anybody in their thirties. Anybody that had more years than I had fingers and toes was seriously the wrong side of healthy living.

Nowadays of course, it is the opposite. The days are so short I cannot do even half of what I have to do, and I am armed with every planning app, every piece of wearable technology. I am organized, but with less time to do too much more.

And worse, I am not alone.

It is the middle of June as I write this and (I kid you not) – I have just seen a TV advertisement saying that it is "only" 160 days until Christmas.

We must hurry. There is no time to lose. Clearly, as I contemplate the summer rain here in June, I should already be searching out the deals on Christmas trees.

But this is not about the ravages of time – it is about how time changes our perceptions of reality, and how, as Barney was growing older into a dog and no longer a "little puppy", – so he was starting to learn one of life's important and sad aspects – that not everybody likes you, and that you cannot trust or smile at everybody. In life, in the same way that the cat will always start to eat your food if you let him get away with it – so there is the gradual dawning of truth that, sometimes, people are lying when they smile at you. Sometimes they do not want to see you.

If beauty is in the eye of the beholder – so a dog is only as cute as the person who is viewing him.

And it happens by accident.

I am running around my home and the dog is following me, eager to help, little tail wagging, a sort of panting breath and a look of total trust and expectation in his upturned face, as if this is Batman and Robin time, and we will "descend into the Bat Cave" and go on another great adventure! – But my mind is elsewhere. I put my shoes somewhere, I have no clue where – oh, yes, I put them outside the back door … And I open the back door.

Sure enough, my shoes are where I obviously last put them, and I gingerly try them on again, and Barney the little Westie sneaks past me when I am not really focused, and he is away.

No lead, no restriction, and in a series of barks and yelps, designed to scare the birds in the trees, Barney is off down the garden, in full "I'm going to protect my property" mode. It is lovely to watch, but not today. I have "things to do", until then, I was busy saving the world, or at least sending emails.

But in that split second, life has changed, for all of us.

I call out to my son, who is languishing in front of his games console. "The dog's escaped!" – I shout out.

"OH F…!" You really don't want to hear this next bit, but let's say that my request for assistance to locate and then round up one stray excited little Westie was less than enthusiastically received.

The response "I told you to keep his lead on," was expected, and similarly … "Well, I'll go down the bank of nettles, brambles, other detritus etc., at the back of the garden, and you stay up here to keep calling the dog!"

Our garden happens to be long – and it does indeed descend deeply into the streets below, via a sort of minefield of brambles that the Stasi in Eastern Germany would have been proud of. I can hear Barney barking in the depths below.

"He's down there!" I shout out. "Barney – good dog! Barney – chewstick! Barney, walkies!"

This is ridiculous. Barney is not stupid. He has already learnt (see earlier chapters) that when Dad says "chewstick" he really means, "God you are SO grounded, it will make Nelson Mandela's confinement seem like a pleasant weekend."

No. I am FREE! And I am chasing a FOX! – Who, I am sure, was here. Just up here … ohh … what's that? Up THERE?

Up until now, this exercise, whilst time consuming and frankly annoying – has all been within our city garden limits, so to say. Nobody else has been troubled. OK, I have had to reach out the hand of friendship and conciliation to my teenage son, but you could argue that this is family bonding and what families do.

But life is a bitch, and has a habit of kicking you when you are down, isn't that so?

The phone rings. I answer, "Hello," I say … I am about to continue with, "Look, I'd love to talk but I'm just a little tied up … etc."

"Is it your little dog in my garden?" enquires the voice. It is my neighbour. Now isn't it a fact of life that the people you live next door to, or just down the street, who are charming and self-deprecating to a fault, suddenly reveal a darker side when your little pet animal is trampling over their flower beds.

She carries on, but this time it is different:

"Richard – I have to tell you. We love Barney as our own." There is a soupçon of tears.

What? I am struggling with this,

"Please tell me you have found him safe and well?"

But this is easier said than done. My son is reporting from the deep, that Barney is nowhere to be found.

I start to descend also into the deep undergrowth. My neighbour is by this time alongside me, albeit the other side of her hedge, and minus her gun.

"I'm sure I heard him down there!" she opines.

And this is the point. The nice little, "coochy coochy coos," of just six months ago from everyone far and wide to this little scrap of a puppy; when they all wanted to cuddle him and smile and say nonsensical baby language – now in the blink of an eye – when it's serious and it is clear we have no intention of taking said puppy back – we risk getting the "this is my property that you are abusing" type of conversation implicit in the "he's such a nice little dog, I'm sure he'll come back – very soon," … words that are actually expressed.

Human body language is a wonderful thing. But this time Barney is not just our family – he is everybody's family. He even gets Christmas cards – from our neighbours. This is ridiculous.

And Barney, too, is beginning to understand the subtle signs. And we are getting worried. It has been over an hour already. Our own tone of voice has lost the sense of anger and annoyance. There is a timbre of genuine concern. Sure, Barney has a little tag, and a phone number, and probably very soon, a police ID number if he is not careful – but Barney alas cannot read. He is not going to wander up to a passerby in the street and say.

"Excuse me, mate (I don't know why he would say 'mate') – my name is Barney, could you just use your cell phone to call my Master?" (I'm not sure he would say 'cell' either … I just thought it would sound a bit mid Atlantic cool).

No. Barney is by this time lost.

Also by this time – my wife and daughter have arrived home; Barney is not the only one in the doghouse. There are some sharp exchanges of looks where no words ever need to be said, and my wife reverses her car, and drives around the corner, back to the streets below our own house, and parks up in the rough lane at the bottom, many feet below. She starts to walk up the lane, with my daughter. They have treats and chewsticks in their hands.

"Barney … chewsticks!" You must be joking.

There is a young family, who are in the lane below, we have never met before. The father is teaching his young daughter how to ride her bike.

"Well, there is a hole in the wire fence, just down here," the little girl says.

By this time, it is starting to get dark. All four people – the two hitherto unknown neighbours, and my wife and daughter, – are engrossed in looking up and down this wire fence. My son has descended more or less to that spot, but on the other side of the wire. And I am managing the military exercise – with my neighbour, who is becoming increasingly anxious before her old man arrives home any minute. I am tempted to call Hereford and the SAS and invite them to do their assault planning at the foot of my garden.

And then it happens. A little mottled face – suddenly appears in the undergrowth, deep at the bottom and by the hole in the fence.

The little girl sees him first, "Look, there he is!" she cries!

And Barney, too, is eager for this game to stop. My son reaches out to pick him up, passes him to my wife who is about to give him the dressing down of his life, when she notices that he is snuggling into her, giving her a lick. There are not the yelps of delight, pink tongue hanging out as usual. I get an SMS on my iPhone; "We've found him."

What is clear is that life has turned a corner. It was all OK when the rabbit escaped several years ago. He only destroyed my neighbour's flower bed once, before the foxes got him later that night.

With Barney, we need a more permanent solution. And Barney knows it, too, his ears go down, he looks away from us, head down. We put him in his bed; shut the door of the utility area.

It is as if there is a coming of age, of adolescence overtaking childhood, or the discovery that Father Christmas is not real after all. But then again, perhaps I am missing the point here. Because after all, apparently we are all supposed to be celebrating him, in 160 days' time.

Chapter Eleven

The shopping trip – Discovering that little girls under two years old are not your friends either

I am sitting having breakfast; it is a lazy Saturday. Saturday is the ONE day off I take in the week. It is not a religious thing. Sometimes I go to Church on Sunday, sometimes I don't. Sometimes I get a guilt trip on a Sunday morning, as I get on my bike and cycle over to my office. I have to cycle through the Church grounds (it's a short-cut).

That's OK at 08.30 in the morning when nobody is there, but by midday – when I am cycling back – I get the full flow of congregation in the process of exiting, as I swish by, trying to pretend I am invisible. I have my gardening shorts on, and a T-shirt that I got from the beach at Navia, Asturias, that has seen better days.

"Richard! Hello! You are looking well!"

That's possibly true, but I have just negotiated the steep hills of Plymouth and I honestly don't know how these people do the Tour de France or can ever make it up the Champs Elysees, but either way – I have to stop and acknowledge the greeting.

"Why, yes! Trying to keep fit, you know, that sort of thing…"

The older man, who is doing his best at friendship, has his even more frail wife by his side and I am seriously worried that she will not make it home, with the look of absence that she gives me. But this is not the time for, "And how are YOU?" conversation.

I speed off.

But this is Saturday. I am trying to find a meaning in all of this. And so I say across the kitchen – "Why don't I take the dog into town?"

My daughter looks at me as if I have just volunteered to travel with Barney to Afghanistan.

"Are you out of your mind?" she looks up.

Now, I have been shopping before and I know that there are little Chi-Chi cafes, etc., in the cafe society that is now the West of England and I thought, well, maybe this is the next step in the growth plan of the little dog.

"You do know that you can't take dogs into Marks & Spencer's?"

Actually I didn't know that. This rather defeats the object.

You also cannot take dogs into supermarkets, or food shops, or frankly anywhere. Apparently you have to tie up your pooch to a railing outside your chosen shop. Sure. I can just imagine Barney being tied up, with that look of confusion, in sort of stilted Andalucian Spanish:

"Why have you left me here, no? Are we not a Team? Did I not say I would come with you?"

So, you go shopping – but you cannot go into any shops. Clearly this is going to give rise to all sorts of long term psychotherapy issues with dog in years to come if we don't get this first session right.

The answer – after several minutes' thought – was pretty obvious. It simply takes two people to go with said dog, into town. One to do the shopping; one to hold the dog. Simples.

"Walkies," I say – and Barney jumps up, goes and gets his lead in his mouth, and runs back to me, expectantly. I open my Volvo driver's door, Barney jumps in the passenger side, and is booted into the back of the car by my son who is elected to ride shotgun on this mission into the unknown. I feel like Captain James T. Kirk, about to boldly go!

"Bones – are we ready? Give me warp factor three!" Even the dog looks at me as if I am quietly barking (pardon the pun, I couldn't resist that one) – but I reverse out of the drive, and we cruise into town.

And Sainsbury's does indeed have little rails where you can tie up your dog. Barney is delighted and sees a little lady Bassett Hound sitting patiently outside. Maybe this is what "shopping" really is. You and I can go shopping in peace – while we leave Barney to chat up the attractive female dog sitting outside. He is clearly happy at seeing the little girl dog, and she likewise. I have no idea what they talk about – but the issue is; I have no wish to go into Sainsbury's that morning. I give a sustained tug on the lead and drag Barney away, but it is a lesson in life that is not lost on either of us.

Shopping with dog is a pulling mechanism, both for dogs – and also for myself. I am stopped by at least three young Mums en-route to the Mall.

"Oh, what a delightful little dog!" I am tempted to go into all sorts of Nick Hornby style narrative and conversation here, but my teenage son who is alongside me gives me a look of disdain. "For God's sake Dad, what will Mum think!"

Why is it that teenagers, who we carefully bring up and educate to have even looser morals than we did in the sixties, have become more prudish, more alcohol-free, more rigid and conservative – than ever we were in our own youth?

"Just being polite; friendly…" I reply.

This is not a convincing argument and Barney, too, is pissed with me for killing his chat-up with the young Bassett Hound.

It gets worse.

We find an open-air street-side cafe and, whilst my son looks after the dog, I go inside to order a cappuccino, a frothy milk thing for my son, and a bowl of water for the dog.

The waitress comes out first with the bowl of water for the dog.

"Oh, what a delightful little dog!" she exclaims. "Can I stroke him?" I am beginning to lose the will to live. It has been at least fifteen minutes and still no sign of my cappuccino or frothy milk thing. Eventually we get the caffeine hit we ordered, and as my son disappears up the street to the Apple Store, I try to look cool, sort of relaxed in the Californian sunshine. A group of young girls, in their late teens are sitting nearby, and I am tempted to relax the dog lead and let Barney wander over.

I do no such thing, and after a lukewarm exchange of smiles, I start to educate Barney about male grooming, House of Fraser perfume departments and designer brands. Barney listens intently, his head cocked to one side, and I am sure that he is taking absolutely everything in. He is sitting by my side as I talk. Every now and then he jumps up on his rear legs to give me a giant lick. I suppose this is what they call "male bonding."

My son comes back, and no, he didn't buy any stuff for his Mac – he went instead to the Game store and got something so violent that only psychopaths or convicted murderers have the right to buy.

"I said that my Dad was over there, and I used your credit card," he says.

Oh brilliant. I am not sure how many years in prison you get for this sort of misdemeanor. We let this episode pass, and decide that maybe we should try Barney in some sort of neutral environment, let's say down by the waterfront, and this has the added advantage that we can pass by a few pubs.

But then the inevitable and unexpected happens. A middle age mum arrives, shopping bags in tow, and three tiny little kids. It is a military exercise.

"Sebastian – just sit there with Beyoncé and Heidi," (where do they get these names from?) – But the girls look adorable and they are all designer dressed even though none of them are more than two years old. Their dresses are pristine white.

There are apparently moments in life when you get that sort of out-of-body experience, where you can see yourself doing or saying things, as if you are watching from a distance, but powerless to change anything. I am sure you know where this is going.

Barney – when he stands on his rear legs – is actually taller than any of the little kids adjacent. The problem, if you will, is that, for Barney, all people are his friends. He has not come across people who do not want to reciprocate the paw of friendship. For adults, this is not a problem, they can simply step aside, and I can restrain the dog lead. But for little kids, whilst we do not want to give them the impression that all animals are to be feared or contained; there has to be some sort of restriction.

The question is – what?

Barney stands up, aware of the fixed gaze from the three little kids next to him. He whines in a high pitched soft way, which is obviously a cry of persuasion.

Against my better judgment, I relax the dog lead, Barney scampers the one or two yards and puts his paws up on the nearest girl's dress.

The little girl is terrified and, with an ear piercing scream, starts to cry.

At this point, their mother appears. I pick up Barney, hold him on my lap, and stroke his chest. Mother placates her daughter. Suddenly there is this invisible barrier between us.

And that's the problem. It is a growing up experience. The balance and the immediate decision-making we all do in life.

"Can I trust you?" "If I open myself to you in friendship – will this be abused or reciprocated?" and, surprisingly, it is harder with animals and young dogs to facilitate this process, than with children. Young kids are usually harnessed in kiddy strollers or whatever, so they are no threat, and the worst they can do is throw their chocolate ice cream all over you. Little dogs however, are not restrained because we have to gently encourage them to interface with society at large. At least that's the theory.

So the risk of things going badly wrong, of people misjudging the moment, is high.

What is clear and becoming clearer every day – for all of us is – not everybody likes little dogs. There is no answer to this situation. We quietly leave, and Barney is already looking ahead. The events of a few minutes ago are seemingly forgotten.

We cross the street and up onto the Hoe and the green grass overlooking the bay, before descending down into the waterfront. The pub at the foot of the steps – is open. We go inside. The waitress serves Barney first. "Isn't he adorable?" she says, "Can I stroke him?"

Chapter Twelve

Sleep time – What to do when the cat sleeps in your bed

There's this great joke from the late and so loved Robin Williams, in one of his stand-up shows at Carnegie Hall in New York. It has become a classic about human behavior:

"If the world was run by women – there would be no wars! Just every 30 days there would be moments of intense negotiations."

God I love that joke!

I first heard this one when watching a video at my friend's apartment in Goteborg, Sweden. We sat on their sofa, and died with laughter. Sometimes the best way of looking at our issues is when we can laugh at ourselves.

Because – apart from the humour – there is the inbuilt truth of what we are hearing.

Yes, it's true. Testosterone filled activity rarely lends itself to compromise. Yet – in society we have to live with each other. There have to be rules, which provide the framework for co-existence.

The problem is, that this is a revelation that is not hard wired into our mind-set. It's something we have to learn as time goes by. We learn from a very young age that throwing a tantrum in the middle of Sainsbury's does not get us any more sweets at the checkout till. Back in the day, this got us a clip round the ear. Nowadays, just in case your three year old phones his lawyer, you get:

"Now, Phoebe … don't scream like that … it upsets people," which of course does nothing to stop Phoebe and everything to piss you off. Harmony is not in compromise. Somebody has to set the rules.

All of which is a learning experience both for Barney – and also for Boh the cat. And it plays out like this, and is related to all parties in this Modern Family growing up.

Barney by this time is getting bigger. He understands the concept of bedtime, and this is reinforced when it becomes clear that already, he can no longer fit into his original soft little bed that sits on the floor of the utility room.

So; we pop down to Beds R Us, or wherever … and we buy the biggest soft bed. We even buy a sort of fluffy 'throw', a sort of duvet cover for dogs. Even the Sofitel at Heathrow does not have beds as comfy as this. Just as a safety check, we buy a new squeaky toy – this will be the inducement – for the dog. OK, so he now has; lovely executive class bed; fluffy cover; and toy. This is like the king size double with the extra pillows and the remote for the TV, built into the bed.

We get home and unpack all this, all the while making stupid remarks like, "Hey, Mr. Puppy, will you love this!"

I don't know in retrospect why we did not take Barney with us to the shop in the first place, he could have tried them all, but we didn't. The moment of trying the bed – is right now.

It is 11.30 in the morning. We spread the fluffy blanket thing over the bed, place the toy in the middle – and look back expectantly. We are still smiling and making stupid noises. Even the cat has come by to see what all the fuss is about is. Boh the cat jumps up onto the fridge and looks down.

Barney the dog stands and looks at the new bed, and then looks up at us.

"Excuse me, this is all very nice, but why are we going to bed?"

There is this confusion in his face, "Did I do something wrong?"

It gets worse. We pick up Barney and plonk him in his new bed. We squeak the little toy. Barney is not remotely interested in the new bed, and jumps out, and walks back into the kitchen. This is not how it goes in all the adverts or movies. I am beginning to wonder how many takes they have to do in the doggy adverts before the dog in question gulps down the protein-rich biscuits or whatever, with a smile on his face. They probably have to starve the poor animal for three weeks to the point where he would have eaten his own flesh if he waited any longer.

"This has just cost us fifty quid!" I say to my wife, who walks away. This is not going to be the best day of our lives. I always knew that doing good in society was a bad idea. Somehow with the best of intentions, we fail to see the possible outcome that it might not be as we had hoped. Or maybe that the concept of "giving", is actually the reverse; we give because we ourselves want to feel good.

But the fact remains; Barney needed a new bed. The outcome, however, that we had definitely not foreseen – was – what to do with the old bed? The cat by this time, who is several years older and QED, that much more astute – definitely knew that this was a social compromise too far. If Doggy is getting a new bed – well, then, what about ME? Boh the cat – who had hitherto remained silent, a disinterested voyeur so to say – started to get vocal.

This was going to be a discussion. It is one thing telling the cat that he has already been fed that morning, so shut up asking for more breakfast.

It is quite another when there are complaints of favouritism that are being hurled about. So, on we go with guilt trip number two. We decide that the cat will have to do with a new fluffy throw, as a sort of compromise. At least it is not another fifty quid.

We get back home again and lay the new fluffy throw over the old doggy bed, which has now been re-allocated as "bed for cat", and this does sort of even things up.

The cat by this time is fast asleep on a chair somewhere in the house. Barney is full of activity. This is not going well. We decide to wait until night, before trying again.

What is becoming clearer as the day progresses, is that, in the same way as all of us as individuals are either "morning people" or "night people" – so Barney is the same. He is not a "morning person". Waking him up at 7.00 in the morning, becomes similar to waking a sleeping teenager. There is a yawn, one eye opens, and a look of total confusion that says, "I am asleep ..." and the eye closes.

And thus at night, Barney is in party mode. We get to 10.30 p.m. and the end of the News and I'm thinking maybe I can watch the football on the TV in bed, and Barney thinks, "yep, great idea", and he follows me up the stairs to bed, and plonks himself on our bed, in front of the TV.

"No," I say... "your bed is downstairs." It is only Arsenal and some second division team on the TV so I get out of bed, physically carry Barney down stairs, and lay him gently in his new bed.

He looks at me, there is no smile on his face. He gives a "humph" ... and rests his head in total resignation, in his bed.

The cat by this time is nowhere to be seen. He has gone out for the night. The bed remains unslept-in. He will come back in the morning, and fall asleep on a chair somewhere else.

And yet, over the next few days and weeks, all parties start to work out this new order of things. Barney knows that late in the evening, the concept of bedtime is significant and he does indeed have his own space. He still follows me up to watch the football on bedside TV, but equally, if we walk towards the utility room, he trots along, places himself happily on his fluffy duvet thing, interests himself in his squeaky toy, and happily falls asleep.

I am beginning to feel like I have negotiated peace in the Arab Israeli conflict. Alas how naive. There is a reason why the cat does not sleep in his newly fashioned bed. And the reason is ... the dog has a much better bed. What on earth would my friends say if I had to let slip that a dog had a much better bed than I?

It is a subtle process, the sly maneuvering of position that cats do so well. Whilst Barney wears his heart on his sleeve – you know instantly if something is wrong. So Boh the Cat places himself by the door, by a chair, or wherever Barney is due to progress. Barney is terrified of the cat, and Boh knows this.

Things inevitably come to a head when Barney, asleep on the sofa – decides to catch up on a few biscuits, and walks in to the utility room to see the cat spread out in his doggy bed. There is this "Woof!" A look of amazement. "What the f…!"

The cat does not move. He opens one eye. And closes it again.

This is a serious conflict. This has all the hall marks of the deep-seated antagonism of Ukraine and Russia. No amount of discussion and diplomacy is going to sort out that one. It is a different level of deliberate obstinacy and aggression. Get this wrong, and you create a precedent for years to come.

The answer, is simple enough. I pick up Barney's bed; give it a shake. The cat falls out, and shakes himself down and walks stiffly away. Barney resumes having some biscuits.

It is a lesson in life, on two levels. The relationship between Barney and the cat is one of tolerance, and on rare occasions, of assistance − but also of antagonism when the mood arises. This is not going to change, and the best we can hope for is friendly and mutual co-existence, sparked by moments of angst.

And on a deeper level, maybe it's that testosterone thing. It's my territory! I wonder what would have happened if both our pets had been female? God I love that joke.

Chapter Thirteen

The car journey – It is true. Life is a big adventure

It's time to go on holiday. And Barney is family. But the most Barney has ever travelled (apart from his first ever trip when I picked him up all those many months ago) – is down to the beach and back – a journey of about five miles tops.

To explain the conundrum briefly, just so you get the broad picture; it is surely the moment for Barney to come travel to London, see the sights, the mass of people, experience the hubbub, and maybe meet some pert London female doggies? Or maybe come on the annual pilgrimage down south on the ferry and car drive, to the beaches of South West France. Entente Cordiale, all that stuff. The last time I went down that way on vacation, they were selling little baby pigs in the local market. Surely a dog in the back of the car will be a piece of cake?

I am alone in this point of view. My son looks up and says;

"Dad, are you out of your mind?"

My wife gives one of those looks and then gives the opposing view.

"If we are going to London, well, it's three hours, and where will Barney go for a pee if we take a train? And if we take the car, we will have to stop at every service station. And you know that Barney does like to socialize – he will want to go and lick everyone, and you know what trouble that got you into last time just in town!"

She continues; "At least on the ferry they have those dog kennels, and if we stop over in France somewhere, it will only be a couple of two hour stretches in the car."

She is right. So maybe there is a glimmer of hope for France.

"But the issue is; honestly speaking – I don't want to go again back to France. Not that it's not lovely, great people, nice ambience, etc. – but we already live near a beach and South West UK actually does have some days when it does not rain, thank you very much. If we are that hung up on sun and beaches, well, what's wrong with what we already have?"

It's a good point. I am losing this discussion.

And yet, Barney is excited beyond belief when it's "Car Time". He has learnt to scamper into the passenger seat. He knows the pub down the road. His ears visibly prick up we get to the Chi-Chi cocktail bars on the waterfront. Barney is a social animal.

So we decide on a compromise. The answer being – let's drive to the regional airport, 40 miles down the road, see the planes arrive, and meet my daughter who is coming back from somewhere. What can possibly go wrong? Bit of a journey, not much traffic, see a few strangers, and see some planes. A sort of "trial-run" for the Big Day that may or may not be in the future, i.e., the transatlantic flight to see friends in Miami – I am getting excited myself by all this. Sounds like a plan.

Because the fact is – Barney and I are becoming great friends. He is good company. I say something like, "how do you fancy going in the car?" and he cocks his head on one side, jumps up and makes for the front door.

Now, part of me has this suspicion that this is like all new born parents:

"Darling! He's just said my name!" – Cue for tears of joy and general weeping etc…

There are these TV sitcoms about newly married life which are deliberately plying this sort of nonsense and the canned laughter sounds, and we laugh, too – because we recognize all this utter stupidity in our own lives.

Except that we don't recognize it in our own lives. We think that. "My God! He really does understand me!"

There is that great scene in *Dirty Rotten Scoundrels* when Steve Martin announces with tears of mock joy; "I can walk! I can walk!" and you and I know he can walk anyway, but it's just the humour of the whole thing, sending up the nonsense of being astonished.

So, on we go. Barney clambers into the passenger seat … yes, OK we've done that bit before, sorry – he rubs his nose up on the window. I wind down the window a little, and Barney pokes his nose out and enjoys the fresh wind as we cruise along the dual carriageway.

This is going to be an hour plus journey when it really should only take 40 minutes. How so? I can't hit the accelerator; this is definitely a 50 mph trip as Barney has decided to fall asleep with his nose over the handbrake and so I drive very sedately, not wishing to disturb his slumbers.

He starts to snore; BIG deep breaths. Then a silence. And then a rumble from somewhere deep. A sort of shudder of the mouth … and the same again. So much for deep bonding and conversation.

We take the ring road around Exeter, and then the slip road off the M5 towards Honiton and immediately the exit for the regional airport. I am telling Barney to wake up.

"Look! There's a plane coming in!" I shout. Barney does not know what a plane is. I use my free hand to point to the sky, where there are two minuscule little white dots approaching from a distance, something like *Close Encounters of the Third Kind*.

Barney is looking at my finger tip – then at me. What on earth is he talking about? Should I be excited? Why should I be excited?

And I am getting stressed. They have moved the entrance to the car park. It used to be just a little drive in – now there is a barrier, and a voice thing and you have to mutter some lines from the third chapter of *The Da Vinci Code* – and then the barrier raises and you try to find a space.

Barney knows about car parks. He knows that you have to get out. He just does not know why? But so far, it has been a great trip. We have at least arrived. Barney jumps out, and the first thing he does is do a pee on the grass. OK, Good BOY!

We find the entrance to the arrivals hall. Now, I don't want to be disparaging about the good people of Exeter, but their airport is not exactly Terminal 5 at Heathrow. My garden is bigger than the whole building. But at least they do HAVE an airport, and here we are.

Some taxi drivers are talking nonchalantly to the lady at the car hire desk. We are early.

Well…I think. Perhaps we can go to the observation platform and see the incoming planes. There is no observation platform and there is only one plane, the 21.05 from Glasgow via Manchester, that my daughter is on.

O–K. Let's maybe go for a little stroll?

Barney is on his lead, but he is scared. He does not want to go for a stroll, but he doesn't want to stay inside either. He wants to go and talk to all the taxi drivers. The taxi drivers are not interested. Barney goes to jump up on his hind legs, "Hi guys; I'm here!" His tongue is out. He is smiling.

No reaction. I drag him away, and we set off up the road along the perimeter fence. Barney finds a quiet spot by the main door and does a poo. I bend down, poo-bag at the ready. There are no bins for the poo-bag, so I think 'bugger' and I leave the poo there, on the grass. Yes I know, I shouldn't have, but what the heck; they should have provided bins …

There is a space by the fence and we are just in time to see my daughter's plane touch down. Even though it is small turbo prop, it seems huge close-up, and the racket is enormous. Barney almost jumps into my arms, but he is strong, and he wants to GO AWAY! He is scared. And I am worried. This was supposed to be a genteel sort of arrival.

I carry Barney back to the Arrivals terminal entrance and the scene is transformed; people are already coming through, and Barney wants to talk to all of them, but he doesn't know any of them and the whole thing is so confusing. He runs up to a young girl who he thinks is my daughter, but he is mistaken. She is not wonderfully happy about it either.

And then the baggage carousel starts up.

This is just too much. There is fear in Barney's eyes, he does not know what this carousel actually does, why is it making this awful noise … he is pressing me so hard, and I am almost shouting, "Barney, It's OK!"

And then he sees some suitcases coming along … he knows what suitcases are; there is a hint of relaxation. And then my daughter walks through … OMG! Thank you, Jesus! Barney dashes, on his lead, and is beside himself with deep joy.

"Oh, Barney! Good Boy!" Barney trots happily ahead of us as we make our way back to the car. My daughter sits in the passenger seat, Barney cuddles up beneath her legs. Who cares about the journey home? He doesn't. Life is back to normality.

I eventually find the car park ticket, the barrier raises, and I return along the airport road and slip into the A303 and M5. I hit the accelerator.

God, it's good to have my car back. Barney is asleep.

Chapter Fourteen

Night life – We are going to the theatre

Sometimes, life just does not fit into place. The chronology of things that should have fitted so well – simply doesn't. Let's say you want a ride into town, and you phone, and say, "Hey, honey, are you going to pick up our daughter in town…" and she says; "Well actually I've just left but I'm already too far gone…" etc.

Now that particular example – is not such a big deal. It happens all the time. Sometimes it works, sometimes not.

There are some evangelical Christians I used to know – that would drive into town, and as they ascended into the multi-storey – would exclaim!

"Yes, God has left us a car parking space!" as they espied a vacant space on the left. And I used to wonder about that and it sorely troubled me.

I mean, I go to Church, too, but how does God know exactly when I am coming up the ramp in my Volvo, when he has 60 million other inhabitants to worry about – and that's just in the UK. Maybe God has some sort of GPS iPad app, that gives a little red glow or something, and he says:

"Yep…just configuring floor number five…there you go!"

No, it can't be.

But then again, there are times when you think – just a few weeks of happenstance, and it would have been so much better.

The local fringe theatre in Plymouth was running the Christmas production of the *Wizard of Oz*. Little Toto the dog was a dead ringer for Barney. Just imagine – a little Westie, mangled hair, cute as cute, strolling on at the end when he is called; "Hey, Todo, (Americans have a hard "t" sound) where are you?" And on he runs…

Except that at that time, Barney, cute as he was – was still only a puppy. The only words he knew even by that time, were:

"Barney, walkies," and "Barney, chewstick!" Even the magical pronouncement, "Barney, breakfast!" was not yet soft coded in his memory.

It could have been so good. Never mind. Life moves on…

Then again, life often moves in big circles, little as we know it. The chance came again just a few months later.

My daughter came home, beaming! "I've got the job of producing the next performance," she cried! And so began a series of evening taxi rides where I was the taxi driver, and Barney the co-pilot, taking and picking up my daughter to and from work.

Except that 'work' finished at 9.00 or later, in the evening. This was a theatre after all. Stuck up a small hill, hidden away in the boutique area of tourist Plymouth, next to the waterfront.

But it became a routine nonetheless, with its share of complications.

First – there was nowhere to park – apart from blocking off the entrance to the walk way across the waterway to the aquarium. And this was a tourist area. Yellow lines everywhere. So you have this Council driven situation where you want to go shopping, support the local small shops, but the nearest you can park your car is a mile and a half away.

Even at 9.00 p.m., there are still queues of people wanting to take the little ferries around the bay – and people already on their third pint leering out of the pub at the foot of the hill.

What the hell. We park the car, block off a few of the people, and Barney gets out of the car, on his lead.

"People! My God, lots of people!" and not just that, a lot of passers-by have nice little puppies, all neatly arranged and obedient.

Barney gives a soft whine, and pulls on his lead. I let the lead relax just enough to test the water, so to say. And it's a funny thing. The little dogs that Barney wanders up to – are just as happy to engage in conversation with him, too. They sniff each other – before their owner sort of smiles and drags them away, up the hill.

Barney looks crestfallen, "What did I do wrong?"

Well, mate – you did nothing wrong. Barney makes a move to explore the balustrade that looks out into the harbour and across to the fishing boats. I have to stop him from walking down onto the gangway and onto someone's private boat.

Yes indeed. You did nothing wrong. It's us as owners that are doing it wrong. Why can't we stop and chat at our level, too, "Hello, my name is Richard... you have a lovely little dog," "Are you just visiting?" or something equally banal.

But it is as if the visitors are bringing their London tube train mentality to this different part of the world – a sort of, "Well, I'm not sure if I really can speak to these people, they might not be British," or whatever.

I once opened a conversation with a young lady standing next to me on the tube from Green Park to Baker Street. She told me I was the first person that had ever spoken to her in all her commuting years. It was a nice conversation, nothing major – and then the doors closed and she was gone.

The problem with all this – is that it establishes a pattern of behaviour. Slowly, Barney stops going up to little dogs that he does not know – to say hello. He registers an interest – a sort of nod in the general direction of the other little dog – but then the moment passes, the doors close, so to say.

There seems to be a growing maturity about Barney as he takes on board all of the zillions of experiences in his little life and files - them away into a logical database. It's a sort of conditional equation: IF little dog runs up to you at the waterfront THEN only go and say hello if the owners seem OK, too … and Dad lets you go.

My daughter jumps into passenger seat; "God it was a packed house tonight," she says, excited! Barney is excited, too. I relate what has happened that day.

"Fancy dropping by the local pub?" I suggest. Barney likes the local pub. They have little dogs there, too, and they are friends. The bar maid serves us a couple of beers, and finds some water in a plastic bowl for Barney. There is no pretention here. There are no tourists either.

Barney falls asleep at our feet, on the new carpet.

"I've got thee tickets for all of us to see the Shakespeare in a few weeks," she says. "Cost 36 quid."

But Barney is already snoring. Maybe he wouldn't have been a very good Toto after all.

Chapter Fifteen

The Inducement – Let us thank God for "Chewsticks"

There are two ways of persuading people to do things. One is by simple persuasion itself. You give a set of options, and people select the one that obviously works best for them, because that's the way you frame it.

The other way is that you simply say; "That's the way it is. Take it or leave it." You can only do that for so long. Eventually, you get to a point where you are no longer in a place where you hold all the cards. And that's when you say;

"I don't give a monkey's f…"

This is not the best solution either, because neither party has anywhere to go.

You find this is in teenage and parent relationships in the worst case; in cultural issues in a modern society; and in divorced couples. By the time you get to that point, there is no room for compromise, there is no appetite for rapprochement, and the result is the "result" if you will, of probably years of resentment. The blow up point, is simply that. It's not a negotiating position and that's the end of that.

The problem here – is that neither of these solutions, works as far as your pet dog is concerned.

First – persuasion itself is lost on the little animal. You try to explain to Barney that if it's a choice of running down the rear garden bank, and then being grounded – OR scampering around the local park and seeing his friend Jessie, the Labradoodle – then surely there's only one answer, isn't there?

Barney cocks his head to one side – and then to the other side, in apparent confusion but with a sort of knowing understanding. Or it may be me; maybe I'm giving Barney attributes that he does not have. I already know that I have a naive understanding of doggy relationships, so nothing would surprise me more to know that I am being hopelessly stupid about this aspect too.

But it's not as if I am expecting some sort of reasoned response from the dog, I mean, he is not going to suddenly talk, and come out with an argument that balances the chances of this, or that, or what if, or maybe I could try this … etc. As much as I love Barney the dog, and as intelligent as I believe he is – this is not a persuasive "discussion". Ultimately, the conversation will end us in the latter camp of options, and it will be.

"Look, this is how it is. You are staying indoors! Right?"

But this is no good either.

There has to be a better way, a sort of middle path, and the answer – when we discover it – is as simple as it is ingenious, and it centres around food, and the relationship between the cat, and the dog. And it starts at breakfast time.

The cat is in the habit of staying out at night, and as I come down in the morning to make the morning tea – so the cat is wanting to come inside. The cat does not use doors or cat flaps. He comes in through the small side window in the kitchen and somehow manages to squeeze his whole body though the little gap between window and frame. He miaows – which is his morning greeting – a sort of, "Well, here we are then, I'm OK – are you OK?"

In reality this translates into, "Shall we do breakfast now?" It is a routine. And it is based around food. The cat has no distinction between being a 'morning person' or a 'night person'. He is a 'food person'.

Barney the dog, however, is most definitely not a morning person.

The kitchen door opens, and he is comatose in his bed. One eye opens … he grunts. He does not move. He watches the cat saunter past him as I get breakfast for both of them. I open the utility room door, there is a flood of daylight and fresh air, and still Barney makes no move whatsoever.

The cat however is getting more vocal. He nudges his head against my arm, as I open his food sachet, and he cannot wait. This is service. God it is even better than the Holiday Inn, where you have to serve yourself.

Now normally, that would be the end of that. I make Barney's breakfast, too, and he struggles to get up, stretches interminably, but really is not yet fully awake, and he sits and looks at his food. This is usually the trick to annoy the cat; stand far enough away from the juicy pieces of meat – but not too far.

He finally stirs himself, eats the food – it takes about 10 seconds to gulp down the lot – and then he decides to go out of doors.

And this is where the problems begin. The cat, meanwhile – has finished his breakfast by this time. He is one satisfied little furry animal. He is licking his lips. He is in concentrated mode. Life is good, God is in his heaven, there is blue sky after night time – and now it is time to sleep.

The problem is that (see earlier chapters) – Barney's bed is on the floor and is the equivalent of a king size executive double which having been only recently vacated is lovely and warm – and the cat's bed is perched up on the washing machine countertop, and is to all intents a single, in an Ibis budget hotel just near Old Kent Road.

There is really no contest, and whilst I am making cups of tea for family and doing things that families do – so the cat snuggles down on the fluffy bed top of the dog's bed, closes his eyes, and is asleep in no time flat.

Meanwhile, the dog is getting bored with all this. He walks around barking at imaginary birds who have every right to be in the surrounding trees – but they are not coming anywhere near him today, and there are no signs of foxes, and well … what to do. Barney decides to cut his losses, so to say. Why not go indoors and see the family. They are always good for a tummy rub, a cuddle, and they have proper beds upstairs, that are truly big, and there is always space for a Westie on the corner of one of those beds, hah!

Barney saunters up the stairs into the utility area, and then sees the cat.

The cat knows he is positioned directly in line between the rear door, and the entrance to the kitchen and the house. The cat smiles, and closes his eyes.

Barney looks at the cat and gives a sharp bark; "Woof!"

There is a difference in timbre in dog barks that I have begun to understand. This one spells trouble. It means that I have to negotiate.

In the old days, it was a standoff; either Option A: I would pick up the dog bed and pour the cat out onto the floor. The cat was not happy about that option. Or Option B; I told the dog to stop being a Wuusse.

Telling Barney to shape up – cut no ice whatsoever, first, he did not understand. And second, he expected me – as the Master – to actually DO SOMETHING! Barney carried on looking at the cat – there was another "Woof!" – and looking at me.

"Well? What are you going do about it? This is trespass. Invasion of my privacy."

The dog is now actually bigger than the cat – but not as Machiavellian. For Boh the cat, this is a chess game. If I do pawn to K4, is he going to do the knight's defence, or something else, hah!

For Barney the dog, this is simply a breach of friendship. Boh is his friend. How could he! Here are two completely different levels of behaviour and motivation.

The answer lies in the bag of treats that are unopened on the kitchen work surfaces. I open the packet and mutter the immortal words;

"Barney, chewsticks!" I hold out the sliver of meaty biscuit. The cat is yawning, Barney cannot resist the temptation, and he slides by the open space and into the kitchen and gobbles up the treat.

"Good boy, Barney!" I pick up the doggie bed, turf the cat out, and he wanders off into the rest of the house.

It all works itself out, but the thought arises that – maybe I am the one that is being played here? It has been nearly a year since Barney arrived and both dog and cat are learning from each other. Sure, Boh the cat has become more friendly and no longer slaps the dog when he feels like it. But also, Barney the dog is learning that, to survive in life, sometimes you have to fight your corner, too.

It is dinner time, the cat is coming out of his day-time siesta, and ready to party. Barney on the other hand has had a great and fulfilling day. He settles down on the floor of the kitchen. The roast chicken that my wife had prepared earlier – sits waiting, on the stove. This is too much for Boh the cat. He springs up onto the work surface. There is a sudden and almighty series of hard barking, a LOT of noise! The cat sits terrified, unable to move, and nowhere near the chicken. Barney runs into the house, very proud of himself. He has saved the family chicken!

The cat looks down, and jumps away, out of the window, from where he arrived earlier that morning.

My wife is thankful and my daughter comes into the kitchen.

"Why Barney! Good Dog!" she cries, "Here – why don't you have a slice of chicken?"

Chapter Sixteen

It's Christmas – Sometimes, other things are more important than you

The build up to Barney's first Christmas, was unusual. For a start – Boh the cat had seen it all before. He insisted on showing Barney how to roll around in the box that housed the Christmas paper. Barney was not convinced he actually wanted to roll around in any Christmas paper. And building a sort of tree for God's sake! Inside a living room? No, this is all too much.

It reminds me of my American friends who once did a Barbecue inside their lounge, in the house they were renting. They ended up having to pay for the whole room to be redecorated. When I asked them, "Why did you do that?" they replied, "Well, it was raining outside, and we didn't want to get wet," – which sort of figured, in a strange sort of way.

Christmas means different things to different people. For some, this is all about the birth of Christ, it is a symbol of renewal, and before I get carried away and become too spiritual, it is a rebirth of our own faith you could say.

For others, it is a time of shopping. There are people I know who buy their Christmas presents for NEXT YEAR, in the January sales some 11 months before.

"But you might even be dead in 11 months' time!" – I suggest.
"Yes, but it was a bargain" – is the response. I really don't get that.

My next – door neighbour gave me a nicely boxed wine cooler for Christmas a few years ago, and I didn't have the heart to say that chez moi, the wine never stays long enough in the bottle for it to be cooled; ten minutes in the freezer, and hit the corkscrew! But it was an ideal present for my brother, and it had a nice well designed box, and surely he would like it. His father-in-law knew about wines apparently – before he died ten years ago.

So imagine my surprise last year when my sister called and said that she had just sent DHL our presents for Christmas, and – OH! She knew we would just love the wine cooler, etc.!

In many ways, at least for adults, Christmas has 'a meaning' – regardless of what that 'meaning' actually is.
For Barney, Christmas had no meaning whatsoever.

First, the door to the garden was now inaccessible; there was this strange tree with flashing lights and funny spikes and it was made of plastic. It was not a real tree, and you could not do a pee beside the tree because everybody put little boxes there that nobody wanted to open – even though they all know who had given the presents; who they were for and what was inside them. Why not just rip the paper off there and then, save the time?

Worse – everybody was nice to each other. Now, Barney was a friendly dog, but usually it was him who opened the discussion, tail wagging, announcing himself with a small leap and big smile.

Having someone else come and be nice first – well it felt strange. Unusual.

But equally, everybody was frantically BUSY! There was no time for cuddles. No time for tummy stroking. No heart to heart conversations, me and Dad, lying on the hallway carpet. It was total mania.

And they kept pointing to little signs and boxes on the wall of the lounge, and every now and then I would get a chocolate something or other, or maybe it wasn't chocolate – I mean it tasted OK – but why now?

And it got worse. Not as bad as some households where Christmas decorating started the day after Guy Fawkes. At least Barney only had to contend with the last two weeks of December, but clearly that was bad enough – it was a month of hassle all condensed into a couple of short weeks, and everybody harassed, busy with all sorts of things, but no time for him, and worse of all – everybody at home at the same time – EVERY DAY!

In short – the first casualty of Christmas for Barney – was "Me Time". The "walkies were fast and furious around the block, with a cursory look-in at the park, a quick run around with his mates, then back into the car – rush to get the turkey, the tinsel, the replacement fairy lights, a new extension lead for said fairy lights, a visit to the printers for the Christmas cards (we are not believers in these email-type of Xmas card), and then a frantic 45 minutes at Sainsbury's getting a replacement bottle of gin, and one of sherry. It takes just five minutes to get the booze; 25 minutes to queue to pay for the stuff, and another 15 minutes to find the car and get out of the car park – and that includes my daughter attaching Barney by his lead, to the doggy rail outside the supermarket entrance; and retrieving him and her again, a half an hour later.

"What on earth kept you?" she says.

"Don't talk about it, please."

In retrospect, I don't know why we have taken Barney. It seemed like a good idea, the familiarization of all things related to a happy period in the year.

But we are all stressed. Barney sits automatically in the back of the car at this point – he has his little ball and toys on the back seat. We head home.

By this time, the tree is up and decorated. It is time to make the paper chains. This requires a process of workflow that most industrial logistics managers would be proud of. We set up a long line of all of us, licking and gluing paper chains, with Barney at the end of the line unraveling them as fast as we try to make them, and Boh the cat sitting on top of my Hi-Fi turntable, looking on, faintly amused.

Barney, eventually, learns to keep out of the way. As usual the chaos does eventually calm down and we do seem to be getting organized. I have this weird thought that maybe Barney would like to come to the Christmas Eve carol service. I don't know why I had this stupid idea, but we agree a compromise; maybe he can come to the little kiddy's crèche service at 4.00 in the afternoon instead. All the little kids will be yelling and crying at the manger and the parents will be stressed and wondering what little Phoebe is doing as she drinks the water in the font – a little dog will make no difference whatsoever.

And then suddenly – it is Christmas Day. Barney is quite bright this morning; no sign of the morning blues of a usual day. I give him his special super tin of food, and a Christmas wrapped bag of doggie treats. Barney has no idea how to open the wrapping paper, so I help him. I feel that this is a bit of a fraud, seeing as the cat has already clawed his way through his own set of small gifts – but Barney is thrilled with his new squeaky toy to replace the "indestructible" one that he tore to shreds over a month ago. There is this sense of happiness that is pervading the ambience, and I am feeling frankly surprised and content.

I start the traditional process of making breakfast, the only time I venture into the kitchen, but my daughter takes over – since a year ago, the family sat me down and said:

"Richard – it's not that we don't like your Christmas breakfasts. It's just that we HATE your breakfasts."

This was said in what is called a spirit of Christian love. And I don't blame them. They are saying a truth that I have known for some time – that there are better people in the family to cook the one sit-down breakfast of the year, and that frankly my gifts lie elsewhere in the pattern of things. And I am frankly relieved, too. As that great song from the Corrs says … "I never really liked it anyway."

Chapter Seventeen

A New Year – And still no snow? You promised me snow, Dad!

I have talked to a lot of non-dog owners in this last year. What has been a quiet revelation and a happy and amazing learning curve for me as a person – has also helped me to see the issues of owning a dog, and the steps of building a relationship.

The first fundamental is that my initial prejudices – were wrong. Not all dogs deposit their hair all over the carpet. Barney doesn't, and he is fastidious about his personal hygiene. He has an awareness of his own body, which bits need to be cleaned, licked, and washed. He has even come to accept that "bath time" is a necessary evil. He has survived a visit to the Grooming Parlor. He has survived two visits to the local Vet, and they are not the same experience.

He knows that little Jessie will still run circles around him whether he looks well-groomed or he looks like a mongrel scruff who forgot to brush his hair.

He knows that he brings a ray of sunshine to me every single time he walks into a room – simply because his wagging tail is a dead give-away that, for Barney – seeing Dad again is the most FANTASTIC moment! Can't be beat.

He is the only member of the family who sits and listens to my piano playing. And I in turn feel obliged to do a better performance. Barney either flops down by my feet at the piano pedals and listens in repose – or he jumps on the sofa, sits up, head cocked to one side, and gives an appraisal of Bach's prelude and Fugue No. 12. And boy, it's a good performance! All the subtlety, the elegant phrasing – the smooth fingering – I am sure he appreciates it all.

I look back from the piano stool; Barney is sitting there, alert. He does not move. I turn round and play some more.

And it's interesting, because, on those days when the music just does not turn out right –Barney jumps down, makes a whiney noise – and sits by the door. I stop playing, and I let him out.

But what is so amazing – is that you can only recognize the inevitability of this process, this unique love-affair, when you take a pause and look back at what you yourself have become, and how there never was any remote chance of this relationship not developing or not working out.

The die was cast the moment little Barney crawled up my leg that early April morning. Perhaps this is what Sartre was talking about – although somehow I don't think so. I don't think he had a little dog in Paris.

Each step of each learning process is as much a learning experience for me, as it is for Barney. He brings a child-like innocence to the table, an openness that is not sullied by our own cynical view of friendship, and that in turn reminds us of what things should be like, rather than what they "are" like.

It reminds me of my friends in Kiev, Ukraine:

"Richard – you live life as it should be; we live life as it is."

But they are wrong. The beauty of human relationships, and now that this includes the optimism that a dog-relationship brings – is what can drive all human nature. It is available for everyone.

And my friends in Kiev know that.

My friend Irina calls me by Skype that evening…she has just been to the local vet, with a small runaway dog that she found sick in the street. She takes him to the vet – she already has two dogs herself and she knows a sick dog when she sees one.

She cannot afford the vet's bill, but she also knows that the said little dog will be put down if nothing is done to save him.

"Irina, that will be HRV500.00 please," says the vet when he has finished.

"Oh, fine! – I'll tell my husband to pop round with the cash in the morning."

Irina is known in the area as a safe pair of hands, a heart of gold.

"Yes, that's perfectly OK," he says.

The vet waits until Irina is safely out of sight and walking home. He turns to his receptionist, picks up the Invoice, and throws it into the bin.

THE END